GEORGE
and RED

The Macmillan Company
Collier-Macmillan Limited, London

GEORGE and RED

by Elizabeth Coatsworth
pictures by Paul Giovanopoulos

with love,
to Uncle George Chester,
a boy in Buffalo in the 1860s

Contents

I

Trouble

That fall of 1860 there was a continual excitement in the air. There were political speeches by day and torchlight processions by night, as elections drew near in the village of Black Rock on the Niagara River between Buffalo and the Falls. Late one evening a whole procession lined up in front of George's house to cheer Papa, who ran a successful flour mill and was an abolitionist and a strong Lincoln man. Papa went to the window and gave a speech. George stood right beside him with Mama and the three girls and saw all the "Wide-awakes" with their torches and yellow oilskin caps, and bowed, too, at the cheers.

People said if Lincoln were elected, there'd be

war with the South for sure, and during the next week Colonel Ellsworth began to drill his Volunteers, dressed in the bright red jackets, baggy blue breeches, and fezzes of the Zouaves.

George and Red were of course there at the drill grounds and George shouted himself hoarse.

"What's the matter with you?" he asked Red. "You don't cheer. Got a sore throat or something?"

"Papa's a Douglas man, and he don't believe in making the South mad. He says if they want slaves that's their business. He says we ought to mind our own business and let them mind theirs."

George thought this over. Minding one's own business was an idea he tried to encourage in his sisters.

"But slaves are different," he argued after a minute. "Slavery's wicked. Papa says so. Why, Mama says more than once there's been slaves right in our house down in the cellar. And after dark Papa rows them across to Canada where they're safe. He can be put in jail for it, too, if the sheriff finds out."

Red was not impressed.

"But my papa don't believe we've got any business making the South do what it don't want to do."

"Well, we have to!" shouted George.

"Pooh, you don't know."

"I do, too."

"You don't."

"Papa says so."

"My papa says no."

"So!"

"No!"

"So!"

"No!"

At this point it was either fight or laugh. It was Red whose wide mouth widened farther to a grin.

Those who had thought that war would follow soon after Lincoln's election were right. George had never seen Papa's face look white until the day when word came that the American flag had been fired upon in South Carolina at Fort Sumter. Mr. Standish sat for a long time with his hands clenched on his knees. "How dared they? How dared they?" he repeated to himself over and over again, and then he got up and opened the chest in the front hall and unfolded the flag, and hung it out; all Black Rock blossomed with American flags that day. But there were a few people who didn't seem to have any.

"Haven't you MacDonalds got a flag?" George asked Red, who looked down and kicked his toe in the road, muttering, "Mind your own business."

George wondered if he'd better say, "It *is* my

business," but he wanted Red to go fishing with him on the river and held his tongue.

Altogether, they were tense days that followed. Men greeted one another with unsmiling faces. "Where will this terrible business end?" they asked. In due time, Colonel Ellsworth's Zouaves, with flowers tied to their bayonets, marched away between cheering crowds. Young men were volunteering, and mothers went about trying to hide their tears. At the Black Rock sewing circles there were ladies to whom the others didn't speak, because they belonged to peace-party families.

The strain made itself felt between the Standishes and their next-door neighbors, the MacDonalds. Mama no longer ran in to borrow a cupful of raisins from Mrs. MacDonald, and Mrs. MacDonald never came to sew with Mama in the parlor. Papa and Mr. MacDonald nodded good-morning when they met, but had nothing to say. Mama even went so far as to remark, "I don't think Georgie should play with that Red," but here Papa put his foot down.

"Leave the boys out of it, Maud," he said. "There's heart burning and back biting enough as it is," and Mama pressed her lips together and said nothing more.

After a while life settled down again. Then came

word that Mason and Slidell, two Southern commissioners bound for England, had been taken off a British vessel in mid-ocean by the Northerners and brought back as prisoners. Would England do nothing when a ship of hers had been stopped on the high seas? No. England, too, would declare war against the North, most people thought. Canada belonged to England, and Canada lay just across the river from Buffalo and Black Rock. The old people began to tell again their stories of how the British and their Indians had burned both towns in the War of 1812. They told of scalped corpses in the snow, of houses deliberately set on fire, and of butchered cattle. They described their own misery, struggling hungry through the woods while the wolves howled.

"And now those devils will be coming to harry us again," the old people declared with quavering fury. A good many other people agreed with them.

"All my lovely silver!" wailed Mama. "My fiddle-back spoons, and the silver teapot and the sugar shaker which belonged to Grandfather Noyes! The Canadians shan't have them, Mr. Standish, if I can help it!" and she and Susan, the maid, spent a day gathering up the valuables and tying them in linen bags to drop into the well the moment they heard that the Canadians were coming.

"Why do you polish every piece, Mama?" George asked, but Mama said she wanted to remember them that way.

"But you'll see them again, Mama," George tried to reassure her. "Even if they burn the house, the well won't burn."

"Yes, but *we* might," wailed Belle, the youngest sister, bursting into tears.

"We mustn't be hysterical, Belle," Annie, the middle sister, declared. "I'm sure if we stand in the front door and ask the officer in charge not to hurt us, he'll be gentleman enough to see that we aren't annoyed."

Yuma Jane, the eldest, but shyest, of the girls, stood wringing her hands. "I'd never dare do that. I'm sure I'll run or faint or scream, or something dreadfully unladylike."

"Papa will protect us, girls," said Mama, crying a little herself as she polished the teapot with a chamois skin. "You can trust Papa completely."

Papa had already taken George with him to Fort Porter at Buffalo. The parade ground was surrounded with vehicles of all kinds, and a long line of citizens were waiting for weapons with which to patrol the river and fight for their homes.

"Can't I have a gun, too, Papa?" George asked as his father joined the line.

"They just issue one to a family, George," his father told him. "I guess if you and Red join the patrol, you'll have to use slingshots."

George had a better idea than that. All the talk about Indians turned his mind to bows and arrows. He had an old Seneca bow (from the Tonawanda reservation) he'd once been given, and now he set about making new arrows, for the old ones were all lost. Red was going to make a bow and arrows, too, because he said anyone had a right to defend Black Rock, even if his papa was a Douglas man. They had quite a time getting the goose feathers they needed, but they managed it in their own way.

"And you needn't be so mad about it, either," George told the goose. "It's for your country, isn't it?"

They split the light sticks they had chosen for arrows and bound the feathers in place, but they didn't know what to use for arrowheads until Red suggested their mothers' veil pins.

"A man gets a big pin, zim, right smack in him, and I'll bet he'll jump in the river and swim right back to Canada," Red said gleefully, and they each took as many big-headed pins as they could find—it was in defense of their country, so they were sure their mothers would be willing, if they knew. A long afternoon was spent splicing them in place. When the boys had six arrows apiece and two bows, they felt sufficiently armed, and began their own patrol. This necessitated playing hookey. Miss Bentley didn't seem to understand and came to see their mamas, but when Mama spoke to Papa about it after supper, Papa backed up George.

"It was wrong of you, George, not to tell Miss Bentley you were joining the militia, but I think in the main you and Red are right. Your eyes are as good as most people's, and better perhaps, and you could see any motion of troops across the river as quick as the next fellow. I tell you what we'll do. I'll write Miss Bentley she's to excuse you for the rest of this week. If the Canadians don't come before next Monday, it's my belief that they won't come at all, and you'll go back to school and make up the work you've lost. Is that agreed to, son?"

In spite of the coolness between the families, Red's Papa sent a note to school, too, and George and Red patrolled the river from dawn to dark every good day and in the rain, too. Their mamas put up lunch for them and they saluted all the men they met on the riverbank—they were always meeting with armed patrols—and they scanned the movement of every cow in the faraway Canadian fields and every buggy

passing along the faraway roads. By the end of the
week England had not declared war, and the anxiety
died down, and on Sunday afternoon George and
Red finished off their patrolling by shooting their
arrows at a bottle placed on a rock.

They never succeeded in hitting it. Something
must have been wrong with the way the feathers were
balanced.

"If the Canadians *had* come, we'd have had to go
right up and stick the pins into them!" George ad-
mitted.

"Yeah! and what would the Canadians have been
doing?" jeered Red.

"Let's not tell about the arrows," George said.
"The kids at school are pretty impressed by our getting excused and patrolling and all. I tell you! Let's
pretend we've been made officers. I'll call you Captain Red, and you'll call me Captain George, and
they'll be green with envy."

For a week or so they did remember their titles and
salutes, and though the other boys made fun of them,
they were quite impressed, and the little girls cast
them admiring looks and at lunch time gave the
heroes cookies from their covered lunch baskets.

But one Saturday morning George got up on the

wrong side of the bed. Perhaps because he, who was usually very cheerful, was feeling cross, everything went wrong. They had liver for breakfast, which he didn't like but had to eat; Belle took the last slice of pie, and he, as the youngest and a boy, had to go without. Then, after breakfast, when Papa had gone off to the nearby mill, Annie tousled his hair in a way he particularly disliked, and then complained to Mama when he tousled hers. Mama had a headache and sat in the parlor with a wet handkerchief over her eyes and was rather snappish herself. Yuma Jane was reading *Ivanhoe* and would say nothing but "uh" when spoken to. And when he wandered into the kitchen, drawn by the smell of chocolate frosting, he found Susan on the warpath.

"No, you don't, George! That's for supper, and your mama doesn't like a broken-into cake, and I don't blame her. You get plenty to eat, if you ask me. Now run along and don't bother me. That's a good boy."

George considered going to call on Papa at the mill. He loved being with Papa, and he loved the river, but Papa had been very quiet and worried that morning. The war news looked bad.

"I don't know where it's all going to end," he had

said, and that was a good deal for Papa to admit.

"Mama, may I take Rex for a walk?"

For once, Mama didn't say "Yes."

"Last time you didn't remember to tie him up afterward, and he chased the chickens. You can't take him again for a week."

If she had let it go at that, George still might have recovered his good humor, but she added something, calling from the next room, after a little pause, "Perhaps that will teach you to be more careful."

George said nothing. He put on his coat and went out, closing the door quietly behind him. He did not frown. He did not mutter. Just the same, he was in a temper.

Red MacDonald was sitting on the steps of his house, whittling as though he didn't have a care in the world. He grinned when he saw George.

"Hi," he yelled. "Been drinking vinegar?"

"You lay off me," said George.

Red didn't guess just what he was dealing with. He pocketed his knife and joined his friend at the gate.

"Old man give you a licking?" he asked with the somewhat jeering sympathy suitable to such occasions. But George was very much out of mood.

"Shut up, will you?"

"Shut up, yourself! Who do you think you are, anyhow?"

It was still just a friendly, independent remark, but at that moment the world looked very black to George and he was not really himself. He lashed out: "At least I'm not the son of a Southern sympathizer." He paused a moment and then added the name of that poisonous snake which in the North meant traitor: "You Copperhead!"

The fighting word had been said. The moment George said it, he was ashamed, but he wouldn't say so. He doubled his fists as Red doubled his. They circled one another, parrying the first punches, and then the fight was on. It was quite a silent fight, too. No one in either house noticed. Rex knew and barked, but then Rex barked for a lot of things, and no one paid any attention to him, except Mrs. Standish, who murmured, "Oh, that dog!" and pressed the damp handkerchief closer to her eyes.

At first neither George nor Red fought his hardest. Each half expected that the other would call it off. They hadn't had a fight for years. But pretty soon they began to get really mad. George punched Red's eye. Red gave George a good whack on the ear, which made his head ring. They were like two fighting cocks now, hitting and grappling and then breaking away to hit again. Panting, puffing, red in the face, they circled and sparred and clinched. They were so evenly matched that it seemed as though the battle would go on forever, but Red made an incautious lunge, and slipped, and George's fist landed square on his snub nose, which began to bleed, and just at that moment, as luck would have it, Mrs. MacDonald flung open the door of the house and called Red in.

"And I should think you'd be ashamed of yourself, George Standish!" she cried, as she slammed the door shut.

George went on down the street. What a world! What a world! He looked toward the Falls. It was one of those days when you could see the mist standing high in the air above the Horseshoe, blowing a little. George thought briefly of the Maid of the Mist. People might see her that evening if there was a moon. Poor girl. They said in the old days, once a year the Indians used to send a maiden over the Falls in a canoe without paddles as a sacrifice to the river. What a way to act! Sometimes George thought about her. All the maidens seemed to share one ghost among them, and all the sacrifices seemed like one sacrifice. But today George's thoughts were distracted by the sound of shots. Someone was after duck on the

far side of Grand Island, or maybe partridge in the
fields. For a moment he tried to place the sounds
exactly, but he didn't really care much. Next he
explored his pockets and found a penny, which he
hadn't known he had. Well, he'd get some licorice
at Benner's. You didn't get much nowadays for a
penny, but he didn't know what else to do. Nothing
was right outside him, and nothing was right inside
him, either. He felt as mean as a bear with sore ears.

At Benner's he bought the licorice stick, and chew-
ing it morosely, started for home. Usually he'd have
saved half for Red, but not today. A beer wagon with
three fine dappled horses thundered by, but he had
no eye for horseflesh this gray morning.

On his way home he had just turned the corner
when he saw a struggling knot of children. Four or
five little girls stood by the fence, squealing with excitement, though Dreena Dayton was crying. Beyond
them were as many boys in a close bunch, hitting at
someone as they yelled "Copperhead! Copperhead!"
The person they were hitting at was hitting back still.
George caught a glimpse of a well-known crest of
bright hair in the midst of the struggle. All the ill-
humor and unhappiness in him rose up like a foun-
tain and broke into sunlight.

"Captain George to the rescue!" he shouted, galloping down the street. "Hold on, Captain Red! I'm coming!" And the tale of the great battle that followed, and the victory of the two against five, was long recounted in the neighborhood annals, and once more George and Red were the heroes of the school, and blandly accepted the admiration of the younger boys and the cookies of the girls.

II

The Princess and the President

It was the fourth year of the Civil War, and the strength of the South was wearing very thin. The North kept pouring in more reserves, but the South had none left. It had little money either, and less credit; food was scarce and so were materials of all kinds. The wonder was that the war went on. But still the South would not surrender. Still, battles were fought and men were killed. George could scarcely remember what it was like before the war, nor think of a world in which there were no marching men or newspapers with flaring headlines. He had made up his mind that he would run away and enlist when he was fifteen. Meanwhile he just went on about his own affairs.

One afternoon, soon after Red and he had begun to go to the Buffalo School, they were given a half holiday to watch a parade. Afterward Red went back to Black Rock because he had something he wanted to do, but George decided he'd go exploring.

George found himself headed toward Scajaquada Creek, passing a few farms and the house of the Indian agent. The Indian village was being moved, and some men were digging down by the brook.

George always gravitated toward any place where people were working. He liked to see what they were up to. It was a fine day in late September, and most of the leaves had turned, but the grass was still a very bright green. Beyond the spot where the men were digging, George saw a chestnut grove, rusty gold, and decided to visit it before he went home, to see if any of the nuts had fallen. Meanwhile he lingered to watch the men.

"What you digging for?" he asked an older laborer as the man stopped to wipe the sweat from his forehead.

"Injuns," he answered shortly. "They want the Injuns got out of here."

Just then the men uncovered an old pine coffin, and as they were hauling it out, the rusty hinges broke. Anxious themselves to see what was inside, two of the diggers lifted the top.

"Well, will you look at that?" exclaimed one with a long whistle.

George leaned over with the others.

There lay the body of a young woman. Her long black hair reached nearly to her knees. She was dressed in a gown of yellow and scarlet striped silk, and there was a silver cross in the hands folded upon her breast.

Everything was bright and strange as George first saw it, and then before his eyes, at the touch of the air, the silk turned darker, and the face and hands changed into dust. The men stood staring rather soberly down at the dead woman.

"She must have been the princess they said was here," the foreman remarked. "Now you see her, and now you don't. Well, we'd better get on to the others," and he reached down and picked up the cross and put it in his pocket.

George didn't mention the matter at home, though he was late and found Mama nearly in tears, as she always was when she thought anything might have happened to George. She didn't worry that way about the girls. After all, she had three of them, and she'd had them longer than she'd had George.

On this particular evening Papa, too, was late, having driven to Fort Porter, where they were advertising a sale of rifles captured on a Southern blockade-runner and not considered suitable for army equipment.

George could tell by Papa's footstep as he came in that he was pleased. He was carrying a rifle carefully over his arm.

"Sorry, Maud, if I've delayed dinner," he said, handing his hat to George. "Look at this. Isn't she a beauty, Maud? A real Belgian rifle."

Mama ran her finger over the polished stock.

"It is a beauty, Mr. Standish. Now wash quickly, for Susan says the roast was ready half an hour ago, and I'm afraid you'll find it burned to a crisp."

It was George who later, by lamplight, examined the new weapon with Papa, lingering over every curve and line of her wood and metal work.

"Aren't you going to load her, Papa?" he asked as he gave the stock a last pat before going to bed, but Papa shook his head.

"I don't believe in leaving loaded guns around," he said. "In fact, I'm so thoroughly against it that I have the bullets for this locked up in the safe at the mill at this minute," and he smiled at his son with complete understanding.

George said, "Yes, sir," but he still felt a passion for the Belgian rifle. He was interested in all firearms, but the blockade-runner's gun was different from any he had ever seen. He wondered if she fired true, what her kick was, whether you had to aim her a little low or maybe high. He wondered about her that evening and all next day in school.

As fate would have it, George came home next afternoon to find everyone out but Susan, and the gun leaning in a corner of the front hall. That was too much. He gave Red the signal cry and sent him off after some gunpowder Red's father kept in the shed. Mr. MacDonald had no bullets that they knew of, but George decided they could use stones. Between them, the boys found quite a few pebbles of a size that would fit the muzzle.

When the arrangements had been made, George put a chalk mark on the side of the barn.

"Just to make sure we don't fire wide and hurt someone," he said virtuously, and they settled down to an afternoon of pure pleasure.

George, as owner's son, had the honor of the first shot. The rifle had quite a kick, and the pebble struck a foot above the mark. Red, having had the advantage of seeing George's miscalculation, got his stone within six inches of the bull's-eye. Bang-bang-bang, turn about, it went. Susan appeared behind them.

"Oh, it's all right, Susan," George said impatiently. "We aren't using bullets," and Susan went off, reassured.

Mr. Standish heard the gunfire as he came up the street, and quickened his step. As he feared, the sound came from behind his own house, and he swung around the building almost on the run.

"George!" he shouted.

George slowly took the rifle down from his shoulder.

"It's all right, Papa, we're not using bullets."

His father's eye swept the neatly painted barn wall peppered with holes of various shapes. His face grew grimmer as a new idea seized him. Wrathfully he strode into the barn, while the boys stood waiting for they knew not what. When Mr. Standish reappeared, his usually calm face was red with rage.

"The new buggy!" he shouted. "You've riddled it! You've ruined it, you little hellions!"

George and Red did not wait to ask questions. Dropping the troublemaking rifle, George turned and ran, with Red at his heels, around the house, past the wildly barking Rex, through the gate, and up the street.

"You boys going to a fire?" asked a neighbor, but they had no breath left for an answer.

At last, nearly half a mile from home, they dared to slow down. George searched his pockets.

"I got an apple," he announced. "We can eat that.

And maybe, sometime, after dark, after Papa's had dinner and Mama's wondering where we are, it'll be safe to go home."

"Do you think it *will* be safe?" Red asked, not convinced. "For you, I mean?"

George weighed the question.

"Well, at least safer," he replied.

As the winter progressed, and the first thaws started streams of cold water running down the hollows of the streets and fields, and the birds changed their calls, there were persistent rumors of peace.

"Sure, that old Lee's surrendered. I know it for a fact. Heard a fellow on the street tell another fellow," Fred Howe, one of the neighborhood gang, assured the others. "We ought to build a bonfire or something."

"Wait till I ask Papa," said George. "You might be wrong."

"How can I be wrong? Ain't I got ears?" the outraged Fred demanded. He had ears sure enough, standing far out on either side of his head. Even George's doubt melted away. Anyhow, a bonfire would be fun. They decided to build theirs between the canal and the river, where the reflections would show up well. A dozen boys scattered to find wood and returned with every legitimate inflammable object they could come on, and a few that looked rather like pickets taken from fences, a small doghouse and a wooden washtub, unwisely left by a back door. By this time their enthusiasm had grown to such a pitch that they would gladly have burned their own favorite possessions.

All up and down the towpath other groups of men and boys were busy heaping up piles of wood in the slush, and there was more than one pitched battle between two gangs for a choice plank or a large fallen branch, and no one had time for supper that night. By now the authorities, too, were convinced, and the church bells were ringing. George heard the big bell at his father's mill chime in. He hadn't known that he hated the war, but suddenly he felt as though his soul were flying up toward the evening star across the river.

Next day they found that it had all been a mistake. Lee had not surrendered. The war was not over. When the rumors crystallized again, the boys were a little more cautious. Still, they didn't want to miss celebrating the victory, and again they built a new fire in the blackened circle left by the old one. But it wasn't such a big fire, although this time the war was really over.

Some days later, on an April afternoon, George was on the streetcar, coming home from school, when a gentleman stumbled in blindly and said to all the passengers, in a choked kind of voice: "The President has been assassinated."

When George pounded up his front steps with the news, his mother and the girls burst into loud sobs, and Susan howled from the kitchen.

"Oh! the poor man!" she cried. "I wish I could lay hands on them that did it!" Papa wasn't home, so George ran on to the mill and rushed into Papa's office. At the first words, Papa got up from his desk and walked to the window looking out on the river, which he loved, as George loved it, but this afternoon he did not see it, nor did he hear the bells now tolling.

"I feared it," he said once. "How foolish of the assassins! Who is left to say 'With malice toward none, with charity for all,' now that he is gone?"

Mr. Standish walked home with George, forgetting to put on his hat and holding George's hand tight, though George was getting to be a big boy. George had felt bad from the moment he'd heard the news in the streetcar, but being with Papa made him feel very solemn as well as sad.

A few days later, when the people knew that the

President's body was to lie in state in Buffalo on its way to Springfield for burial, the schools were dismissed so that the boys and girls could join the long, silent line of people come to pay their last respects to their leader. In the confusion George found himself separated from Red, and from his own family, too. The line moved very slowly. Many men as well as women were crying as they waited. But at last George came in sight of the coffin. Four soldiers stood on guard, one at each of its corners. They stood like statues. Not so much as a muscle seemed to move. Only their eyelids now and then flickered as the strain of their fixed stare became too great.

George, always interested in soldiers, regarded these four with an attention as fixed as their own. He had always expected to be a soldier himself, and now that the war was over he supposed that he never would be. It must be a great honor to be chosen to guard a dead President! He wondered what they were thinking about and how long they had been standing. He wondered what would happen if a fly lighted on one of their noses. Suppose it were summer, and a bee should sting a man. Could he stand still? If George were on guard, and a bee stung him, would he be able to stand still?

As he came abreast one of the soldiers, it seemed to

him that the man was looking at him. But he couldn't be sure. It might be like the eyes in pictures, which appear to follow a person around a room. Then it seemed as if the flicker of the man's eyelid was almost like a quick wink. Surely George was mistaken! He glanced quickly at the second man. Again he had an impression of being watched. He looked at each in turn. He saw a muscle moving like a pulse in the cheek of one of the guards. Did the man know it himself? George wondered.

He was halfway to the door before he suddenly realized something. He tried to turn back, but a soldier motioned him to keep his place in the line.

"What's the matter, sonny? Forget something?"

Forget something? George certainly had! But he couldn't say right out what it was he had forgotten, there in the presence of the coffin and everything. He'd be ashamed to tell anyone what he'd forgotten. He was kind of ashamed to admit it even to himself, but the truth was that, in the excitement of looking at the honor guard and thinking about them, George had forgotten to look at—Abraham Lincoln.

Anyway, a lot of people here had seen the President, but George was the only one who had seen a dead Indian princess who could vanish away, like a puff of smoke in the wind.

III

The Dollar

It was a day in early June in 1866. The war was long over, and Lincoln had been dead for more than a year. George and Red seldom thought about him or about the old campaigns anymore. In the warm sunlight George was lying on the mill wharf, watching the river through the cracks. It ran so fast and so clear! He thought he might see a sturgeon go by. George watched and watched. He liked to watch anything alive; he liked to watch any machinery. In fact, George enjoyed watching.

Usually Red did, too, but Red had gone to sleep, curled up in George's skiff, rocked just a little by the current. The older the boys grew, the more of their spare time they spent on the water. They swam,

fished, and rowed up and down the river. They knew
all the eddies and crosscurrents, and how to use them
in fighting the fierce downward sweep of the water.

It was dangerous. A broken oar or bad handling
might bring a boat over the Falls, with the rowers as
helpless as the Maid of the Mist. Papa saw to it that
the skiff carried extra oars, but beyond that he left
the boys alone. "A boy's got to learn by experience,"
he told Mama, worried about her only son. "George
is learning by experience."

"But I'm so afraid he'll be hurt," Mama cried,
with clasped hands.

"He has nine lives, like a cat," said Papa dryly.
But neither Mama nor George knew with what a
careful eye, as he went about his work, Papa watched
George and his doings from the mill.

Red's people left him alone, too. Red's papa and
George's papa had talked it over, in one of their chats
across the dividing fence. Mrs. MacDonald and Mrs.
Standish were having tea together again, or on warm
afternoons, lemonade on the veranda. They probably
shook their heads over giving the boys the run of the
river, but what the boys' papas said, went.

On this warm afternoon, George's drowsy watching of the water was suddenly interrupted by hurried
steps coming down the path and onto the dock. The

steps came to where George was lying and stopped. He rolled over and sat up. The man standing over him was young. He had black, shaggy hair and gray eyes, and wore old blue army pants. George knew at once that he had been a Northern soldier.

"Could you kids take me over to Grand Island?" the man asked.

George didn't answer at once. He liked the look of the stranger, but he was in too much of a hurry. Yet, after all, why not?

"We will for a dollar," he said slowly.

"All right, where's your boat?" The man didn't boggle at the dollar, although when the ferryman was around, he charged only twenty-five cents. This young man was a stranger, or perhaps he didn't care.

George woke Red. "Come on," he said. "This man's going to give us a dollar to take him over to Grand Island."

Red looked surprised. A dollar was a whole lot of money. He took his usual place in the skiff. They put their passenger in the stern.

"Sure you kids can do it?" the man asked. "I want to fetch up on the Island, not at the bottom of Niagara Falls."

"We can do it," George answered briefly, and kept his breath for rowing. Red and he had been on the

river so often together that they worked almost like
two hands of the same body. They crossed the harbor
at an easy clip, warming up while their passenger
fidgeted. The man seemed taken aback as the current
gripped them and swung them sideways and downstream.

"Sure you can make it?" he asked again. "I got to
get there in a hurry."

"Yes, sir," said George.

After a while the stranger seemed to relax, when
he saw that the boys really did understand their
business. He began to whistle "John Brown's Body"
through his teeth, and then a jig, tapping time with
his foot. He was excited about something, or nervous.
George could see that.

"Let me off here," said the man, as they neared
the head of the island. He seemed in an awful sweat
to get ashore.

George looked briefly over his shoulder at the
creaming shallows. "Have to go farther down. We'd
swamp here."

"I'll wade, then," said the man starting to get out
of the skiff without even taking off his boots.

George cried, "You forgot the dollar!" The man
gave a smile which lit up his thin face. "I'll not be
robbing you of your dollar," he said, and tossed a

silver one into the bottom of the boat, where it fell with a loud and pleasant thump.

"Thanks, Mister!" the two boys yelled after him. They bent to the oars again to cross back without too much loss of headway. As they rowed, they saw the man wade to dry land and disappear from sight.

Once across the river, the boys were in no hurry for the final pull upstream. They found a good tree to tie to and did some fishing with the lines they kept handy in an old cigar box. They fished for a while without much luck and as they moved on, they heard shots from the Canadian shore.

"Lot of duck shooting today," Red said. "Do you suppose our man was going hunting?"

"He might have been, at that," said George. "Sure did seem in a hurry."

There certainly was a lot of shooting on the river that afternoon. The boys had never heard so much, but they had their own business to attend to in getting up the current. It was a long pull, but they beguiled the time by planning what they would do with the dollar they had earned.

And all the while they heard the sound of shots from the Canadian shore.

As they at last rowed into the little Black Rock

harbor toward the mill dock, George was surprised to see his father waiting.

"What are you boys doing on the river when there's a battle going on?" Papa shouted as they made their landing. "I've been worried sick over you."

The boys' mouths dropped open. "Battle?" they repeated. "We didn't know there was a battle."

"You didn't, eh?" asked Mr. Standish, still sharply. "Didn't you hear the firing? What did you think was going on?"

"We thought they must be shooting duck," George answered truthfully.

Papa stared at him and suddenly threw back his head and laughed. "That's a good one," he said. "Duck shooting! Haven't you heard about the Irish Fenian expedition? Well, after all, I've just heard about it myself, and there seems to have been no harm done. Why were you boys out, anyhow?"

They told him about their passenger and the dollar, and Papa nodded his head. His anxiety was over now. He assured them with a straight face: "You boys may hear from this, aiding and abetting armed rebellion. Your passenger must have been going to Grand Island to join the Fenian expedition. Their main body crossed the river two days ago and captured Fort Erie from the Canadian garrison. They're led by a crazy fool named General John O'Neill. General! With a few hundred wild Irishmen planning to capture Canada and free it from Britain! They expected the Canadians to join with them, but the Canadians won't. The whole scheme is harebrained and will make bad feeling on the border. Most of the men are ex-soldiers from our army, egged on by agitators in Ireland, and they're going to find themselves in pretty hot water. So, no doubt," he added grimly, "will you."

"Do you think they'll hang us, Papa?"

Papa considered this. "No. A jail sentence, I should think."

Red said anxiously, "But we didn't know."

"Ignorance of the law is no excuse," said Papa.

"But we're not grown-up yet, Papa," chimed in George.

Papa weighed this. "I should think they might take that fact into consideration."

Chattering nervously, the two boys followed Papa into the mill and up into the square tower over the river. Most of the hands were gathered at the windows watching, but they made room for Mr. Standish and the boys.

"Now," said Papa, "we have grandstand seats for the battle. And as regards that other matter, I don't think you need worry. I was only teasing you. But next time, look before you leap."

George and Red gaped at Papa in astonishment. Teasing? Why, they had almost seen the prison bars about them! A weight lifted from their hearts, and they breathed more deeply.

George sighed unconsciously. "We're lucky," he said. "We've got a dollar."

Red gave an answering sigh. "Sure," he agreed, "we've got a dollar."

Next day more accurate accounts began coming in, and people learned what had really happened. On June first, eight hundred Fenians had landed in Canada. The Toronto Volunteers had fought them at Ridgeway, ten miles up the lake, and the Fenians soon began retreating back to Buffalo. The shots that George and Red had heard had been the last part of this battle. Their Fenian must have been one of the latecomers.

During the evening an American gunboat, the *Michigan,* steamed slowly downstream from Lake Erie and anchored offshore, like a sentry. Fenians escaping from the Canadian side were taken aboard, and there was a good deal of talk about what would happen to them.

At school George showed the dollar, which

was passed from hand to hand and looked at with respect. It had been carried in the pants pocket of a real live Fenian. Like as not he was dead now. One boy offered George a dollar and ten cents for the dollar, but George shook his head.

"No, thanks. We'll keep the Fenian money, won't we, Red?"

George had to cut the grass that evening and was pretty busy when Red eased up. The lawn mower made such a whirr George didn't even hear Red till he came right up and spoke to him.

"Say! The small boats are going out to the *Michigan!*"

It took George a while to take that in. Then he looked toward the house. No one was at the window, not even the girls, not even Susan.

"Guess I'll rest my back a little," and with elaborate nonchalance he strolled through the gate with Red.

Once out of sight of the house, they ran lickety-cut for the mill dock, jumped into the skiff, cast off, and rowed out to the *Michigan*. Sure enough, there were a dozen small boats under her counter, and the rails were lined with men, a few of them armed guards, but the others obviously Fenians. Some of the people in the small boats had brought loaves of bread, which they were tossing up to the prisoners. Most of them were caught in midair, but now and then a loaf fell back into the river, where it was seized upon by the current and carried bobbing and twisting away toward the Falls.

George and Red rowed all around the *Michigan* three times before they saw their Fenian. He was staring down into the water, looking at nothing.

"Hi!" Red yelled, but at first the man didn't look at them. When at last he realized that someone was speaking to him, he gave a start and grinned.

"Hello," he said. "Here are the ferrymen."

Red spoke right out what was in his mind. "What will they do to you?"

"Don't know, kid."

"Hang you?"

The young man shrugged his shoulders. "Maybe."

"Anything we can do?" George asked.

The Fenian shook his head. Then he thought of something.

"You might bring me some bread. We don't get much to eat on this ark."

Evening was coming on, and the lawn was only half cut, and it wasn't always easy to arrange about getting a loaf of bread, but the boys didn't falter.

They recognized the voice of duty and rowed back to the dock in record time.

Then there was the walk home and a talk with Susan, which became a talk with Mama, too, and ended with their departing with a loaf of bread, some milk in a covered tin, and what was left of yesterday's leg of lamb. George had also provided a length of fishing line with a sinker at one end to be used for hoisting up food that couldn't be thrown.

They returned more quickly than they had come, but by the time they reached the *Michigan* it was almost dark. The lights of the scattered farms on the Canadian shore were beginning to show. Their man was still at the rail.

"We've brought you some things," George said. "We can't throw the milk and stuff up on deck. You'll have to haul. Here come a fishline and sinker! Look out for them."

George had a good aim and a strong arm. While Red steadied the boat, he threw the sinker with the attached line. They came down on deck with pleasing accuracy on the very first throw, and the Fenian hoisted away at his end. First the meat, then the milk, then the bread, went over the rail.

The man's voice was different when he next spoke.

"Good night, boys, and thank you. This will put heart in me."

From that moment the boys were as busy as a pair of birds feeding fledglings. They begged from the Standish and MacDonald kitchens every spare bit of food that they could get. They even stole a new cake, which Susan had left on the windowsill while the frosting set. When both kitchens were closed to them, and their mamas declared there wasn't another extra bite in the house, they took to buying food with the Fenian dollar. When that was gone, they earned money running errands, burying garbage, whitewashing fences, and even, for one afternoon, tending a neighbor's baby.

Their Fenian was a sharer, and never kept for himself anything like all the food they brought him. They gloried in his generosity of spirit, but it certainly kept them on the run trying to victual the whole *Michigan*. Of course there were others bringing food, too, and now less was needed. The most extraordinary thing was the way the crowd on board seemed to be melting away.

"There's a lot of fellows I haven't seen lately," said Red one evening as they rowed back from their daily expedition. "Have you noticed, George? Do you suppose they're sick?"

An awful idea came to George. "Maybe they've hanged them."

"Not that," said Red, "or our Fenian wouldn't be so cheerful. He was whistling today."

Next evening when the man tossed back the line he said, "I put something on the end of it for you."

He tried to aim the sinker at the boat, but he wasn't a very good pitcher, and it went overboard. However, George hauled it in so quickly that the writing wasn't too blurred to make out. When they got it home they read:

> *Dear boys, You've been very good to me and I'm grateful. Could you be off the stern of the Michigan at twelve o'clock tonight and oblige a friend? P.S. When you get in place, please make a sound like a duck woke out of sleep.*

"But we go to bed near nine," said Red.

"All the better for us," declared George. "We'll go to bed quick, blow out our candles, and later creep downstairs barefooted and meet outside your house at eleven."

"How'll we know what time it is?"

"By the town clock striking."

"Yes, but suppose I go to sleep? I almost never hear that old clock."

"You can't go to sleep tonight," declared George.

When George guessed it was about half past ten, he got dressed and crept his barefooted way downstairs. The creakings of the steps, the soft opening of the front door, wakened no one. There was no moon. The world seemed enormous.

Rex barked and came out of his white kennel, leaping and wagging his tail. George patted him and quieted him in whispers. Papa slept on.

Papa was not the only one to sleep on. Red must have been sleeping, too, for there was no figure at the MacDonald gate.

"Just like him!" thought George furiously. "If it wasn't for me, nothing would ever get done."

He selected pebbles and began to toss them one by one at the windows in Red's room. It took dozens of pebbles before a sleepy voice called, "Hey, wait a minute!"

It seemed a long time before the MacDonald front door opened and Red slipped out. Together the boys walked along the middle of the dirt road, stepping lightly.

Even on the road leading past the mill to the dock they walked carefully, so as not to call Lame Mulligan's attention to themselves. He was night watchman at the mill, an old, sour, sandy-colored man.

They didn't want him asking questions.

But luck was with them that evening. They walked as unnoticed as cats. The oars were in the skiff. They untied the painter and began rowing across the harbor, just as the clock struck again.

"We're late!" said George.

"We're early!" said Red.

They counted the heavy strokes. There were eleven of them. They had an hour to wait. They drew the skiff up in the shadow of the breakwater and waited, whispering and whispering.

When they thought they had waited nearly an hour, they rowed out into the river. Even now, there were still some lighted windows in the town.

"Can you make a sound like a duck, Red?" George hissed.

"Sure," said Red. "But we've got to wait till the clock strikes twelve."

That last wait was the longest and the most shivery of the evening.

"Now!" said George.

Red began to giggle helplessly.

It was George who made a sound a little like a disturbed duck. The first time he made it the noise was so low that no one could have heard it ten feet away, but the second time he squawked louder, and almost immediately they saw a dark shape detach itself from the gunboat and leap into the water.

A voice cried, "Who goes there?"

A shot was fired with a spurt of flame, a voice or two could be heard, but the boys had no time to think of what was happening on board. Their business was with the water. They weren't river-bred for nothing. They had heard the splash, they knew the currents, and bending to the oars, they arrived at the right spot in time to haul their Fenian into the safety of the skiff.

He came over the gunwale, choking and spitting water, but he was all right.

"I certainly am obliged to you kids," he said. "They're dropping off the old ship every night like ripe apples, but you stand a chance of getting drowned if you haven't friends like you to stand by."

"And of getting shot, too," said George, who felt thrilled at having been under fire.

"Shucks, no," said their Fenian. "The guards shoot into the air. I guess they've been told to kind of wink at escapes. In another week, there won't be a Fenian left on the old *Michigan*."

They were inside the breakwater now.

"What are you going to do?" asked George.

"I don't know," said the man. "I look like a tramp, and I need a sleep and a shave, and a dry suit of clothes. But I'll bum along somehow. And thank you both kindly. You boys have been good friends, God bless you!"

When the skiff was tied up, the Fenian shook hands with them as he said good-bye. His hand was wet, and he was shivering, though he didn't speak of it.

George had been struggling with himself. Surely they had done a lot for their Fenian. They'd fed him and helped to rescue him. That was enough, wasn't it?

But George was just discovering that helping weaves a rope of obligation. Their Fenian needed help still, help tonight and maybe a job tomorrow. George straightened his back with a jerk. He'd have to knock at the door and waken Papa. Mama would cry, and Papa might give him a licking. By now it must be one o'clock in the morning, and George was tired and cold. For a moment a licking loomed large. He wanted to say good-bye to their Fenian and slip up the stairs as unnoticed as he had slipped down them, and get safely back into bed, and forget the whole business.

But he couldn't do it. What if he got a licking? He could take it. He didn't know if he and Red had done a good thing or not, helping a prisoner to escape from the *Michigan* in the middle of the night. The *Michigan* belonged to the federal government, didn't it? Yes, but wasn't this a little like Papa's helping slaves escape along the Underground Railroad? Would Papa think so too, or was this different? All right, if Papa thought a licking was coming to him, let it come. Whatever Papa decided about George, he would almost certainly help the man.

It took George a little time to think this all out, but when at last he spoke, his voice was steady and casual.

"You come along home with us," he said. "Papa will fix you up somehow. He's against what you Fenians did, but Papa would help anyone in trouble —well, almost anyone. You'll see."

And together they walked up from the dark river, Captain Red on one side of their Fenian and Captain George on the other, each feeling in his different way that now at last the war was really and truly over— once and for all.